The CRANKY Ballerina

BY ELISE GRAVEL

BLEH.

KATHERINE TEGEN BOOKS
An Imprint of HarperCollins Publishers

She puts on her pink leotard that's waaay too tight.

And her big, fluffy tutu that's waaay too itchy.

She gets in the car and puts on her seat belt.

Every Saturday, Ada gets cranky. That's because on Saturdays, Ada has her ballet class.

Miss Pointy makes all of the girls practice their pliés, their jetés, and their arabesques.

But Ada won't practice hers.

Miss Pointy calls on Ada. "Let's see your pirouette!"

Ada gets into fourth position.

Miss Pointy is trying to be nice. "It's okay, Ada. Let me show you again."

Ada takes a deep breath, closes her eyes . . .

Ada starts pirouetting . . .

. . . out the door

. . . into the hall!

And . . .

"Excuse me, but do you think you could do that again for my class?"

Ada looks at the man. He doesn't look like a ballet teacher. He is dressed in some kind of pajamas.

I GUESS SO.

She takes a running start.
She jumps! She spins!

KICK!

SWOOOOOS

BING!

"This is Mr. Chop's School of Karate. We meet here every Saturday. Would you like to sign up for the class?"

What's this spreading across Ada's face?
Could it be a

For Marie

Katherine Tegen Books is an imprint of HarperCollins Publishers.

The Cranky Ballerina. Copyright © 2016 by Elise Gravel. All rights reserved. Manufactured in China.

No part of this book may be used or reproduced in any manner whatsoever without written permission except in the case of brief quotations embodied in critical articles and reviews. For information address HarperCollins Children's Books, a division of HarperCollins Publishers, 195 Broadway, New York, NY 10007.
www.harpercollinschildrens.com

ISBN 978-0-06-235124-1

The artist used Photoshop to create the digital illustrations for this book. Typography by Martha Rago

16 17 18 19 20   SCP   10 9 8 7 6 5 4 3 2 1 ❖ First Edition